WALT DISNEY'S

Storybook Friends

Peter Pan and Wendy

The Seven Dwarfs Find a House

Cinderella's Mouse Friends

Alice In Wonderland Finds the Garden of Live Flowers

GOLDEN PRESS • NEW YORK

Western Publishing Company, Inc.
Racine, Wisconsin

Library of Congress Catalog Card Number: 75-34634

PETER PAN AND WENDY, copyright 1952 Walt Disney Productions. Adapted from the Walt Disney motion picture "Peter Pan," based upon PETER PAN by Sir James Matthew Barrie, by arrangement with The Hospital for Sick Children, London, England. Copyright 1911, 1921 by Charles Scribner's Sons. Copyright 1939 by Lady Cynthia Asquith, Peter L. Davies, and Barclay's Bank, Ltd. Published 1911 under the title "Peter and Wendy," 1921 under the title "Peter Pan and Wendy," and in 1950 under the title "Peter Pan." ALICE IN WONDERLAND FINDS THE GARDEN OF LIVE FLOWERS, copyright 1951 by Walt Disney Productions. CINDERELLA'S MOUSE FRIENDS originally published as CINDERELLA'S FRIENDS, copyright 1950 by Walt Disney Productions. THE SEVEN DWARFS FIND A HOUSE, copyright 1948, 1952 by Walt Disney Productions.

Peter Pan and Wendy

Once upon a time there were three children: Wendy, John, and Michael Darling. Every evening, after they got into their night clothes, Wendy told her brothers exciting stories about Peter Pan.

Peter Pan was a boy who had decided never to grow up. He lived in faraway Never Land, a magic place filled with adventures and fun.

John and Michael Darling enjoyed hearing about Peter. Sometimes Peter himself, with the fairy Tinker Bell, would fly down to the Darling's window and listen.

One night Peter invited the children to go along with him to Never Land. First he taught them to fly. It was easy, for all that was needed was a wish and a pinch of pixie dust —and a little practice, too.

When they were all ready, out the window they flew and away to Never Land. This strange and lovely place was an island in a nameless sea. There, fairies lived in the tree-tops. Animals roamed the forests, and in a village on a cliff an Indian tribe made its home.

Mermaids swam in the lagoon in the nameless sea. But floating upon it was a shipful of pirates—wicked ones, with an especially wicked leader who had a gleaming hook instead of a hand. His name was Captain Hook.

When Wendy, Michael, and John reached Never Land, they loved it at first sight. Before long they met the Lost Boys, who lived in Peter's underground house, a wonderful place with many hidden doorways.

But Peter and the Darlings and the Lost Boys spent little time in that house. There were too many exciting things to do outside. Sometimes they played with the Indians, who were their friends. Sometimes they had trouble with the pirates, who were their enemies because Captain Hook had a grudge against Peter Pan.

One day the pirates stole
Princess Tiger Lily of the
Indian tribe. Her father, the
Chief, feared that he would
never again see his daughter.
But Peter rescued her and took
her home. This made Captain
Hook angrier than ever at
Peter and his friends.

One night, when Peter was away, the wicked Captain tied up Wendy, John, Michael, and the Lost Boys, and took them off to his pirate ship.

"Now, my fine friends," said Captain Hook when he had them on board, "which will it be? Will you become pirates? Or shall I make you walk the plank so that you will fall *kerplash* into the sea?"

"I guess we'll turn pirates," said the Lost Boys.

But Wendy would have none of that. "You should be ashamed of yourselves," she said. "Peter Pan will surely rescue us."

Wendy was right, for the fairy Tinker Bell saw what had happened, and she flew off to get Peter Pan. He arrived just in time.

After Peter had beaten Captain Hook in a clashing sword fight, he freed his friends. The frightened pirates jumped overboard and rowed hastily away in their boats.

"Hurrah!" cried Peter. "Now the pirate ship is ours!"

"Where shall we sail to?" asked the Lost Boys.

But it was time for Wendy, John, and Michael to go home.

"If you must go home, we'll sail there," said Peter.

They got aboard, and with a wish and a pinch of pixie dust, they made that pirate ship fly! Swiftly they sailed across the sky and back to the nursery window.

It was still dark in the nursery...how could they have gone so far and done so much in just one night?

They never saw that magical land again, and they thought no one would ever believe in their adventures.

But Wendy and John and Michael knew that their memories of Never Land were true. And, when they grew up and became parents, their own children believed in Peter Pan. Don't you?

The Seven Dwarfs Find a House

Once upon a time there were seven little men. All day long they worked deep under the ground in a dark and gloomy mine, looking for bright and shiny diamonds.

At night they slept in hollow trees or in rocky caves, in nests of leaves or wherever they were. They had no place to call home.

These little men were great friends. Their names were Doc and Grumpy and Happy and Bashful and Sneezy and Sleepy and Dopey.

They were the seven dwarfs.

There came a time when the dwarfs grew tired of this
way of living, and decided to have a home of their own.
They wanted soft beds to sleep in and a kitchen where they
could cook their meals.

Their animal friends knew the forest well, so the dwarfs
asked them to find a house for seven little men. Soon the
old owl discovered a little cottage where seven big badgers
had been living, but the badgers had moved away.

Off through the forest marched the seven dwarfs, singing a merry "hi, hi-ho!" And the animals went before them
to lead the way to the empty little cottage in the woods.

Doc went in first, and the six other dwarfs followed him. They all thought the cottage was a fine place to live.

At once the dwarfs began to clean house. Sneezy went to work with the broom, but the dust from the sweeping made him go "Katchoo!"

As for Sleepy, he headed for the beds—seven in a row—and lay down. When Doc came for him, Sleepy was deep in dreams.

Grumpy looked about, sure he would find something wrong. But finally even he had to admit that the cottage was quite perfect.

"Wash time!" called Doc.

This surprised the dwarfs. They had never bothered with things like soap and water and baths. But Doc said, "No supper till all hands and faces are clean."

So the dwarfs washed in spite of themselves.

Happy began to cook, and Bashful stirred the soup. Before long, supper was ready. At last the seven hungry dwarfs sat down to a meal in their own house.

The supper was delicious, for Happy was a good cook. Even Grumpy enjoyed it, every last bite.

Later the dwarfs begged him to play a song, and at last Grumpy sat at the organ and gave them a jolly tune. What a lively time they had, playing, singing, dancing till long past their bedtime.

Then off they marched to sleep in the seven little beds, in their very own house in the woods.

Cinderella's Mouse Friends

It was morning. At the first notes of the bluebird's song, Mouse Town woke with a squeak and a yawn.

The tiny town was hidden in the attic of Cinderella's house, and today was a happy day, for it was the day of the great Mouse Ball. Everyone was busy. All the mice were making the town pretty. The bluebirds, too, were helping as they joined in a merry song:

"Cinderella, Cinderella,
Is the sweetest one of all.
Now she's marrying her prince, and
So we're having a great ball!"

The decorations were well in hand. Jac Mouse was taking a band of some mice to Cinderella's kitchen to find food for the party. Jac was the Town's leader.

"Watch out for the cat!" the bluebirds called.

"We will," the mice promised. They knew evil Lucifer Cat only too well. Squaring their shoulders, they marched bravely away and disappeared into a secret hole in the wall.

Down, down, down, through dark tunnels in the walls they made their way. At last they reached the big kitchen. "Sh!" said Jac, as he crept out to look around.

There, curled up in a cosy spot close to the fire, they saw Lucifer Cat. He was fast asleep.

"Come on!" Jac signaled his friends, and out they crept.

Now the mice were all set for a climb. One, two, three, up to the chair!

Then four, five, six, onto the table. There each one picked up a big load of food.

Then six, five, four, down to the chair! Three, two, one, down to the kitchen floor!

On their soft little feet, the mice crept back, back, back toward the hole in the wall.

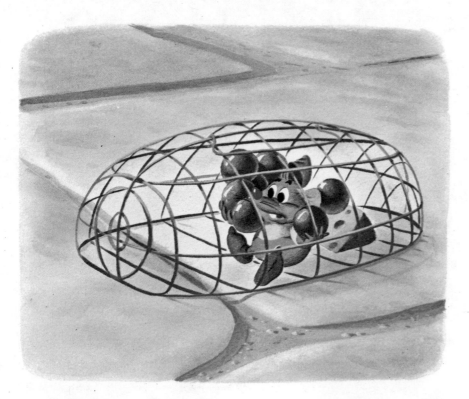

But that plump and greedy mouse Gus spied one more piece of cheese. He couldn't pass it up.

As he reached the cheese, *snap!* Gus found himself locked in a mouse trap.

Lucifer the cat heard the *snap*. He opened one eye, and saw poor Gus.

"Aha!" purred Lucifer with a horrid, hungry smile, and he tried to get at Gus. But the trap was shut tight.

"Someone will soon be along to open it," said Lucifer. "I might as well have a nap while I'm waiting."

"Zzzzz," he snored. And out from their hiding places, hush-hush-hush, the other mice crept softly. They shook their heads at Greedy Gus. Then, one, two, three,

they

opened

that

trap!

And out came Gus. *Ping!* went the trap as it closed behind him.

Lucifer woke up with a start. "Aha!" he snarled. "I've got you now!" And he sprang, his sharp claws shining! "Hurry, friends!" cried Jac. "Every one of you into the wall!"

The mice ran to the wall, carrying all they could. But Jac stayed behind to draw Lucifer's attention from the others. Soon he was leading the cat a merry chase.

Into the hole in the wall the others climbed, each with a load of food. But Gus, carrying a load of grapes, saw that Jac was in trouble. Lucifer was getting closer to him, and Jac was getting tired.

Then clever Gus dropped a grape and stepped on it. Grape juice squirted out and hit Lucifer in the eye. While he screeched, into the wall went Jac and Gus.

Then, up, up, up inside the walls climbed the happy band of mice. As they went, they sang this happy song:
"*Cinderella, Cinderella,*
How we'll celebrate tonight!
We will feast and dance and frolic
By the moon and candlelight!"

And they did. Mouse Town had never been happier than it was that night. There had never been a greater feast—everyone danced and sang until the sun rose.

And that's how Cinderella's mouse friends celebrated her wedding to the prince.

Alice In Wonderland Finds the Garden of Live Flowers

Once upon a time there was a little girl named Alice who was just about your size. Suddenly one day a strange thing happened—she fell down a hole into Wonderland and became very tiny! In fact, she was only three inches tall!

At first Alice liked being a wee little thing. She could sit on a little chair made from a matchbox, and she could carry a flower leaf for a parasol.

But soon Alice became unhappy, for everyone she met was MUCH bigger than she. She grew quite lonely; and so she set out to find someone to play with.

Alice walked through tall grass that seemed like a forest to so small a girl. On she went until she heard voices floating through the air from somewhere up ahead.

She hurried toward them, and soon she reached a beautiful garden.

But there was not one person—big or little—to be seen.

"I wonder where the voices came from," Alice thought. "There must have been someone in this garden."

Just then some odd-looking creatures flew by. "What curious butterflies!" Alice exclaimed.

To her surprise, a voice answered, "They are bread-and-butterflies." Alice looked, but saw no one.

"Bread-and-butterflies! Why so they are," she said, for the little creatures' wings were slices of buttered bread.

Then there came another sound. "It's a horsefly buzzing," she said.

But the same voice corrected her. "Can't you see that it's a rocking-horsefly?"

When Alice looked toward the buzzing sound, she saw a winged rocking horse swaying on a leaf!

"You are right," she said to the voice. "But may I ask where and who you are?"

"I am Miss Rose, of course, and I am right here," the voice answered.

At that moment Alice saw the face of the Rose watching her. "Oh!" said Alice. "I didn't know that flowers could talk."

"Of course, we can talk," a proud Iris sniffed. "If there is anyone we care to talk to."

"But the flowers I have known have never had a word to say," said the tiny girl.

"Chances are their beds were too soft," said a Morning Glory. "When flower beds are too soft, flowers sleep all the time."

"Do dog-and-cat-erpillars live in your garden?" asked a Dizzy Daffodil.

"No, I wish they did!" said Alice, stooping to pet one. "I like it here. May I stay?"

"What garden are you from?" a Daisy asked.

"Oh, I don't live in a garden," said Alice.

The flowers stared. What kind of creature could this be if she didn't live in a garden?

The clever Tiger Lily thought he had the answer. "She must be a weed!" he said.

"We want no weeds here!" cried the Pansies.

"No weeds!" cried the Rose, reaching her sharp thorns toward Alice.

"No weeds! No weeds!" cried all the other flowers.

Then the dog-and-cat-erpillars began to bark and hiss at her, and the dande-lions roared. Poor tiny Alice was so frightened that she ran away as fast as her little legs would carry her.

"Oh, dear," she thought when she was back in the forest. "I do wish I were my own size again."

She sat down to rest and think.

"Who-oo are you-u?" said a voice beside her.

Alice looked up to see the haughty-looking fellow who had spoken. He was a caterpillar, puffing on a water pipe and blowing the most elegant smoke rings Alice had ever seen. The smoke rings formed words as he spoke.

"Who-ooo are you-u-u?" he said again.

"I'm Alice," Alice said. "At least I think I am. I've changed so since this morning that I'm really quite confused."

"Exactly what is your problem?" asked the caterpillar.

"I really would like to be larger," said Alice.

"Why?" the caterpillar asked.

"Three inches is an awful height," said Alice.

The caterpillar drew himself up angrily. "I am exactly three inches tall!" he said, frowning. And he puffed on his pipe till the smoke hid him from sight.

When the smoke cleared away, the caterpillar had quite disappeared. Only his pipe and slippers were still there.

Poor Alice felt stranger than ever. "He won't be any help to me after all," she sighed, feeling close to tears.

Just then a voice buzzed and buzzed in her ear, "My girl, I have something to say to you."

It was the caterpillar's voice. "Anything can happen in Wonderland," it said.

"Where are you?" said Alice, looking all around.

"Anything," said the caterpillar's voice. But it was coming from a butterfly that hovered nearby.

"Why, you've changed, too," said Alice in surprise. The butterfly who had been the caterpillar nodded as he swooped away with a sudden flap of his wings.

"I suppose anything CAN happen here in Wonderland," Alice thought. "But HOW does it happen?"

All at once, she began to grow taller and taller, until she was back at her own height, just about your size.

Alice was very pleased. "I like this better," she said. "It's nice for bugs and flowers to be tiny, but I would rather be just me."